The Little Red Hen

Retold by Vera Southgate M.A., B.COM
with illustrations by Mélanie Florian

LADYBIRD TALES

ONCE UPON A TIME there was a little red hen who lived in a farmyard.

One day the little red hen found some grains of wheat.

She took them to the other animals in the farmyard.

"Who will help me to plant these grains of wheat?" asked the little red hen.

"Not I," said the cat.

"Not I," said the rat.

"Not I," said the pig.

"Then I shall plant the grains myself," said the little red hen.

So she did.

Every day the little red hen went to the field to watch the grains of wheat growing.

They grew tall and strong.

One day, the little red hen saw that the wheat was ready to be cut.

"Now the wheat can be made into flour," said the little red hen to herself, as she set off for the farmyard.

"Who will help me to take the wheat to the mill, to be ground into flour?" asked the little red hen.

"Not I," said the cat.

"Not I," said the rat.

"Not I," said the pig.

"Then I shall take the wheat to the mill myself," said the little red hen.

So she did.

The little red hen took the wheat
to the mill and the miller ground it
into flour.

When the wheat had been ground into flour, the little red hen took it to the other animals in the farmyard.

"Who will help me to take this flour to the baker to be made into bread?" asked the little red hen.

"Not I," said the cat.

"Not I," said the rat.

"Not I," said the pig.

"Then I shall take the flour to the baker myself," said the little red hen.

So she did.

The little red hen took the flour
to the baker and the baker made it
into bread.

When the bread was baked, the little red hen took it to the other animals in the farmyard.

"The bread is now ready to be eaten," said the little red hen. "Who will help me to eat the bread?"

"I will," said the cat.

"I will," said the rat.

"I will," said the pig.

"No, you will not," said the little red hen. "I shall eat it myself."

So she did.

A History of
The Little Red Hen

The Little Red Hen is an old folk tale. Some sources say it originates from England, while others suggest it is from Russia. Regardless of the tale's history, it has continued to be passed down over the centuries, and it remains as popular today as ever.

The tale has changed little over the years. Its simple narrative teaches that if you work hard, you will be rewarded. The story depicts a hard-working hen who plants the grain, tends to the plants and cuts the wheat all by herself. It is she, alone, who takes the wheat to be ground into flour and baked to make a loaf of bread, without the help of her farmyard friends.

As such, after all her hard work, the little red hen is rightly the only animal in the farmyard to enjoy the bread.

Ladybird's 1966 edition, retold by Vera Southgate, has ensured the tale continues to reach a new generation of readers.

Collect more fantastic
LADYBIRD 🐞 TALES

Cinderella

Hansel
and Gretel

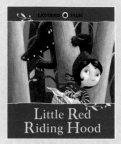

Little Red
Riding Hood

The Three
Little Pigs

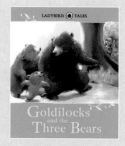

Goldilocks'
and the
Three Bears

The
Gingerbread
Man

Snow White
and the
Seven Dwarfs

Rapunzel

Rumpelstiltskin

Sleeping
Beauty

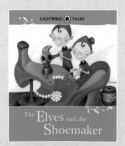

The Elves and the
Shoemaker

Puss in Boots